It's picture day today!

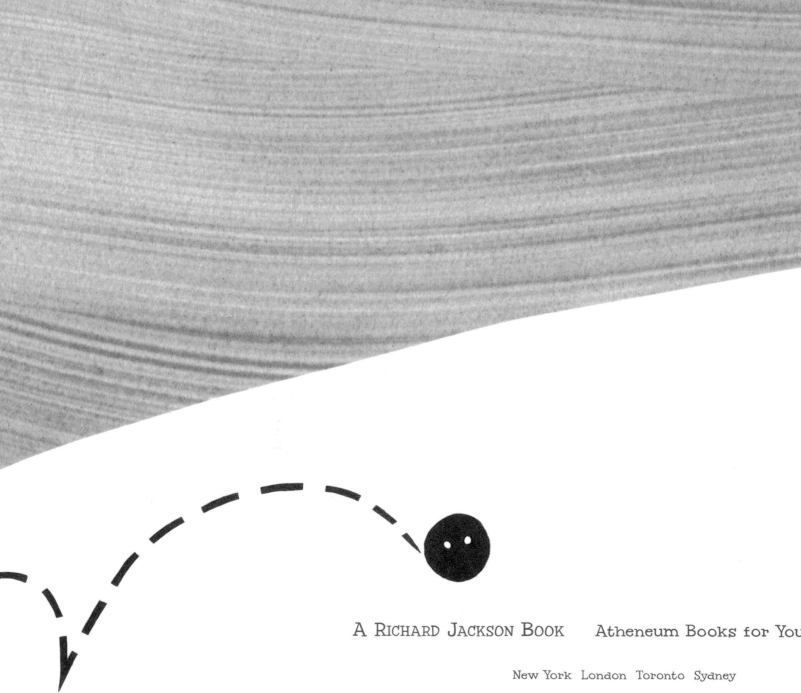

A RICHARD JACKSON BOOK   Atheneum Books for Young Readers

New York London Toronto Sydney

It's picture day today!

by megan mᶜdonald and katherine tillotson

For Katherine
—M. M.

For Megan, with gratitude for this playful story,
and for Dick and Ann, both of whose artistry shines
throughout these pages
—K. T.

Here come Buttons,

followed by Feathers.

Look!
See String?

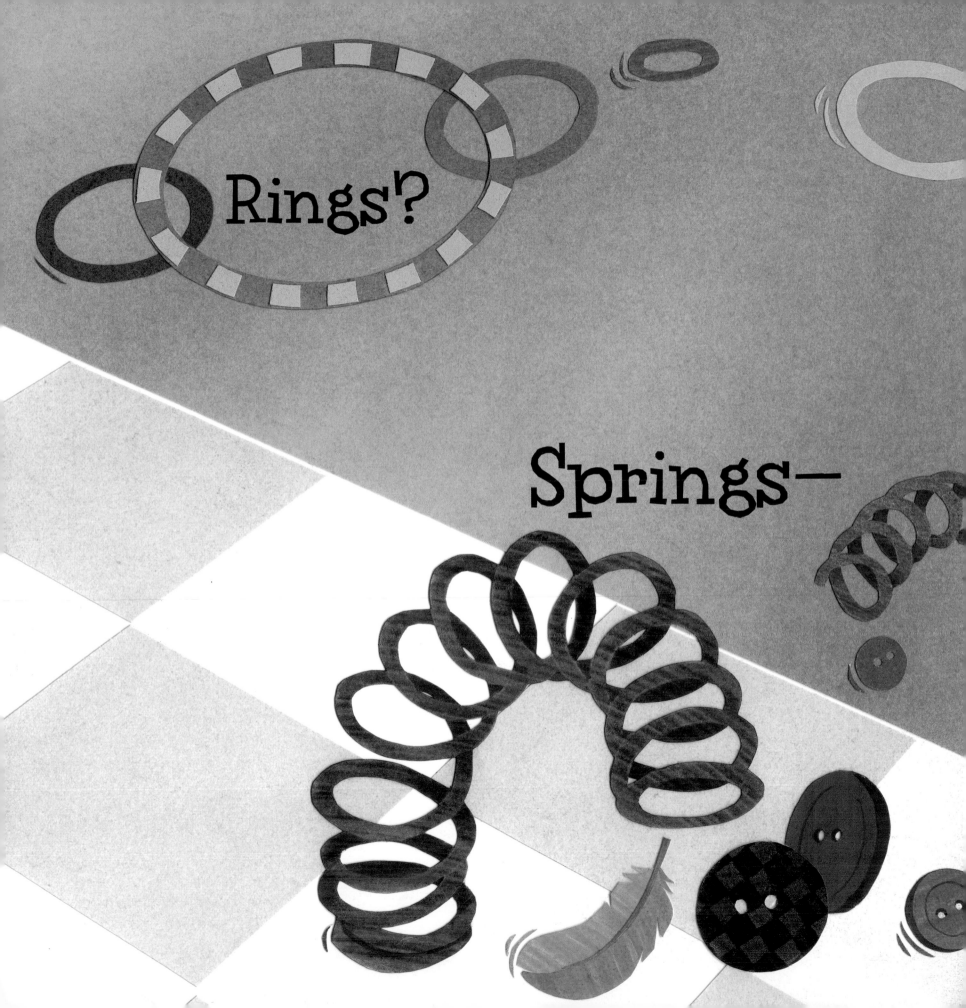

Rings?

Springs—

and wouldn't you know,

the Wheely Things.

Sequins,
Squiggles,
Glittering Stars,
Fuzzy Pom-Poms,
Twisty Yarns.

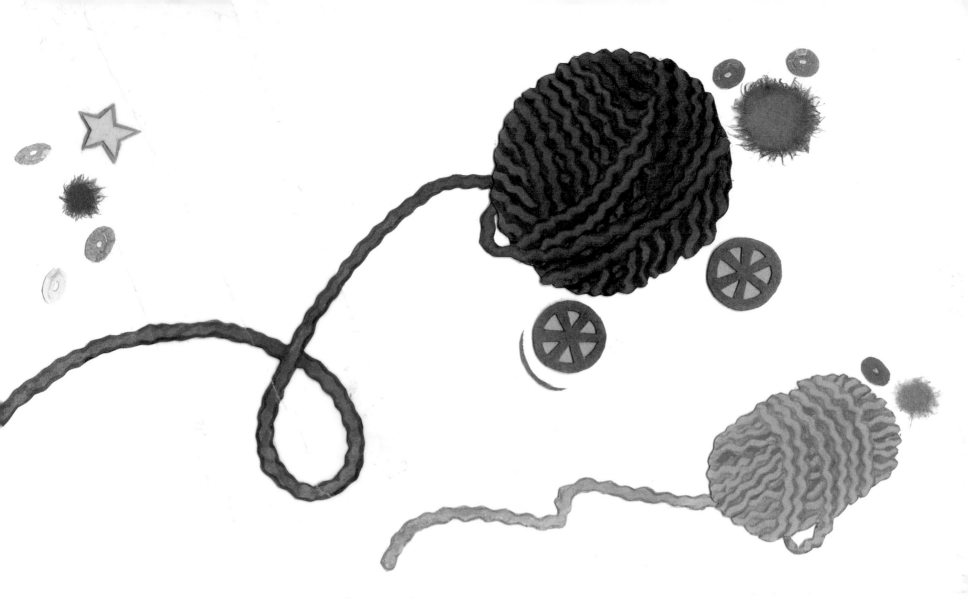

Couldn't keep any of them away. . . .

Hey, it's Picture Day today.

Clothespins?

"Here!"

Ribbons?

"We're here too."

Easter Grasses?

"Yeah."

Odd-shaped Glasses?

"Yup."

So . . .

Who's

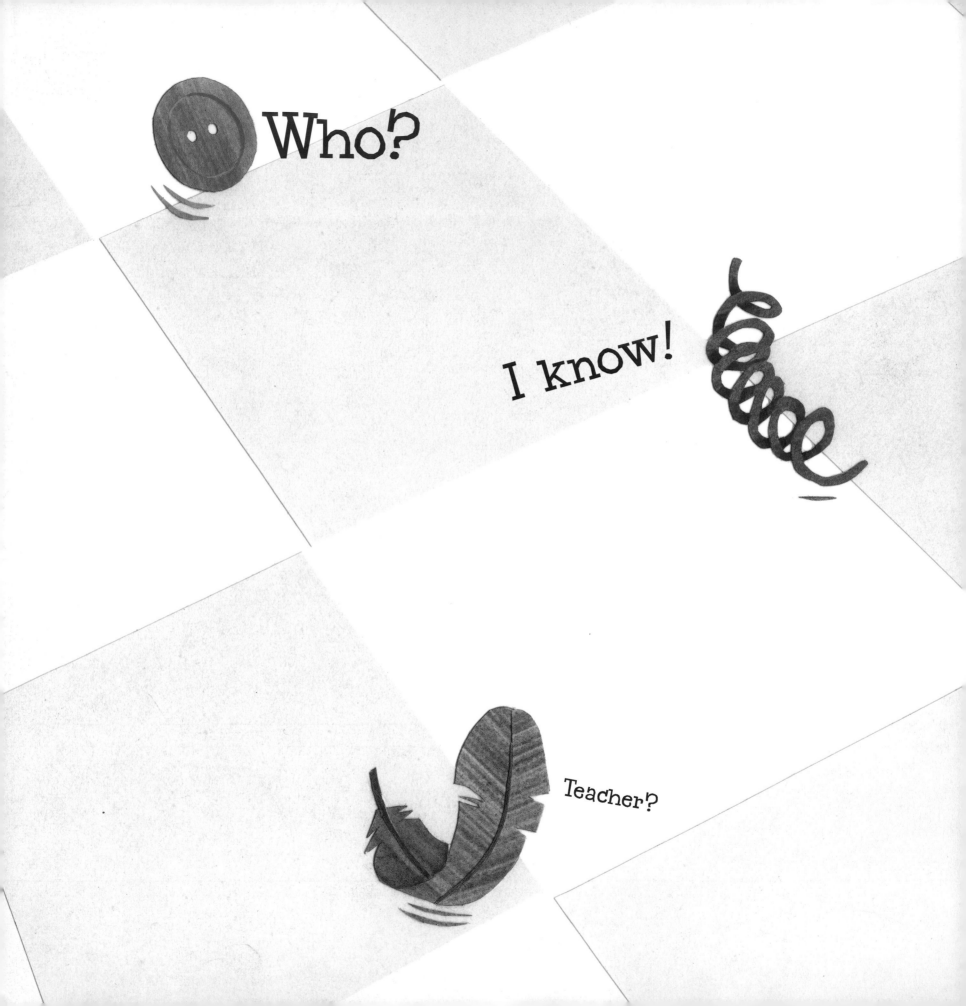

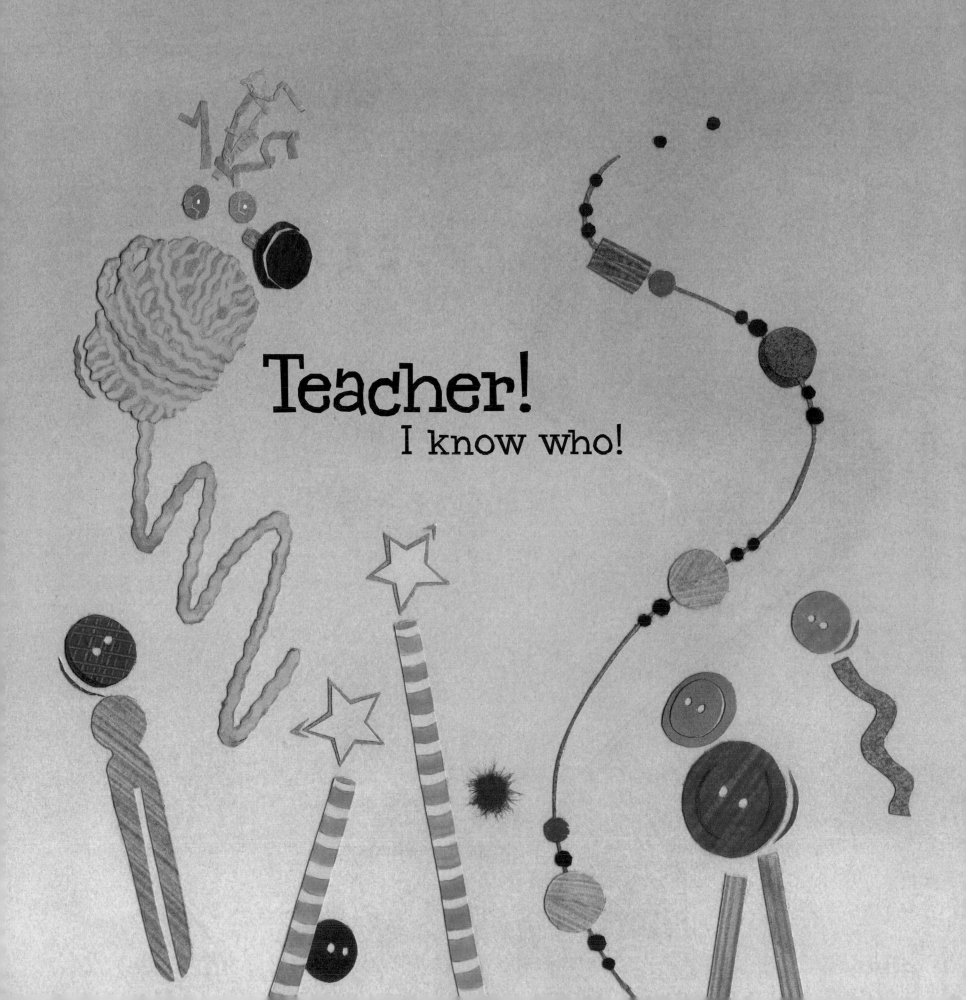

Teacher!
I know who!

"Whew," says Glue.

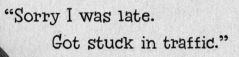

"Sorry I was late.
Got stuck in traffic."

Atheneum Books for Young Readers

An imprint of Simon & Schuster Children's Publishing Division

1230 Avenue of the Americas, New York, New York 10020

Text copyright © 2009 by Megan McDonald

Illustrations copyright © 2009 by Katherine Tillotson

Book design by Ann Bobco

The text for this book is set in Jellygest.

The illustrations for this book are rendered in cut paper.

Manufactured in China

First Edition

2 4 6 8 10 9 7 5 3 1

Library of Congress Cataloging-in-Publication Data

McDonald, Megan.

It's picture day today! / Megan McDonald ;

illustrated by Katherine Tillotson. — 1st ed.

p. cm.

"A Richard Jackson book."

Summary: A classroom of art supplies gathers for their picture day.

ISBN: 978-1-4169-2434-0

[1. Artists' material—Fiction. 2. Schools—Fiction.] I. Tillotson, Katherine, ill. II. Title. III. Title: It is picture day today.

PZ7.M478419It 2009

[E]—dc22

2007046435